HENRY

JAMES

PERCY

Based on *The Railway Series* by the Rev. W. Awdry

Photographs by David Mitton and Terry Permane for Britt Allcroft's production of *Thomas the Tank Engine and Friends*

First American Edition, 1994.
Copyright © by William Heinemann Ltd. 1993. Photographs copyright © Britt Allcroft (Thomas) Ltd. 1992. All rights reserved under International and Pan-American Copyright Conventions. Published in the United States by Random House, Inc., New York. Originally published in Great Britain by Buzz Books, an imprint of Reed International Books Ltd., London. All publishing rights: William Heinemann Ltd., London. All television and merchandising rights licensed by William Heinemann Ltd. to Britt Allcroft (Thomas) Ltd. exclusively, worldwide.

Library of Congress Cataloging-in-Publication Data
Mavis.—1st American ed. p. cm. "Photographs by David Mitton and Terry Permane for Britt Allcroft's production of Thomas the tank engine and friends"—T.p. verso. "Originally published in Great Britain by Buzz Books…London"-—T.p. verso. SUMMARY: When Mavis, a new diesel engine, fails to listen to Toby's advice, she runs into trouble with the mischievous freight cars.
 ISBN 0-679-86044-4 [1. Railroads—Trains—Fiction.] I. Mitton, David, ill. II. Permane, Terry, ill. III. Awdry, W. Railway series. IV. Thomas the tank engine and friends. PZ7.M44587 1994 [E]—dc20 93-23328

Manufactured in the United States of America 10 9 8 7 6 5 4 3 2 1

Random House New York, Toronto, London, Sydney, Auckland

MAVIS

Random House

Mavis is a diesel engine who works for the quarry company, shunting freight cars in the sidings. She has six small wheels hidden by sideplates just like Toby's.

Mavis is young and full of her own ideas. She loves rearranging things, too, and began putting Toby's freight cars in different places every day.

This made Toby cross. "Freight cars," he grumbled, "should be *where* you want them, *when* you want them."

"Fiddlesticks," said Mavis, and flounced away.

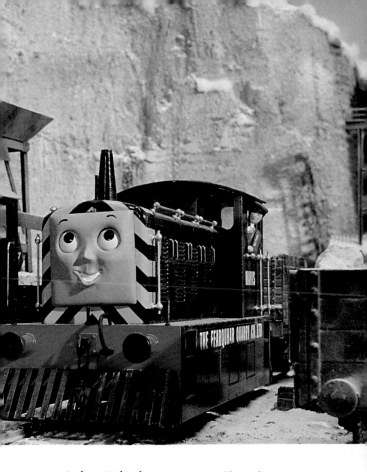

At last Toby lost patience. "I can't waste time playing 'Hunt the Cars' with you. Take them yourself."

Mavis was pleased. Taking freight cars made her feel important.

At the station, Diesel oiled up to her.

"Toby's an old fusspot," she complained.

Diesel sensed trouble and was delighted.

"Toby says only steam engines can manage freight cars," continued Mavis.

"How absurd. Depend upon it, Mavis. Anything steam engines can do, we diesels can do better."

Diesel knew nothing about freight cars, but Mavis didn't realize this.

Toby's line crosses with the main road behind the station and, for a short way, follows a farm lane. Frosty weather makes the muddy lane rock-hard and very slippery.

Toby stops before reaching the lane. His fireman halts the traffic at the crossing, and then he sets off again. By using the heavy cars to push him along, he has no trouble with the frosty rails in the lane. It is the only safe thing to do in this kind of weather.

Toby warned Mavis and told her just what to do.

"I can manage, thank you," she replied. "I'm not an old fusspot like you."

The freight cars were tired of being
pushed around by Mavis.

"It's slippery," they whispered. "Let's push
her around instead.

"On, on, on!" they yelled.

Mavis took no notice. Instead, she brought the cars carefully down the lane and stopped at the level crossing.

All traffic halted.

"One in the headlamp for fusspot Toby," chortled Mavis.

But Mavis had stopped in the wrong place.

Instead of taking Toby's advice, she had given the cars the chance they wanted.

"Hold back, hold back!" they cried.

"Grrr-up!" ordered Mavis.

The cars just laughed, and her wheels spun helplessly.

Workmen sanded the rails and tried to dig away the frozen mud, but it was no good.

Everyone was impatient.

"Grrrr-agh!" wailed Mavis.

Toby was in the yard when he heard the news.

"I warned her," he fumed.

"She's young yet," soothed his driver, "and…"

"She can manage her cars herself," interrupted Toby.

"They're your cars, really," his driver replied. "Mavis is supposed to stay at the quarry. If Sir Topham Hatt finds out…"

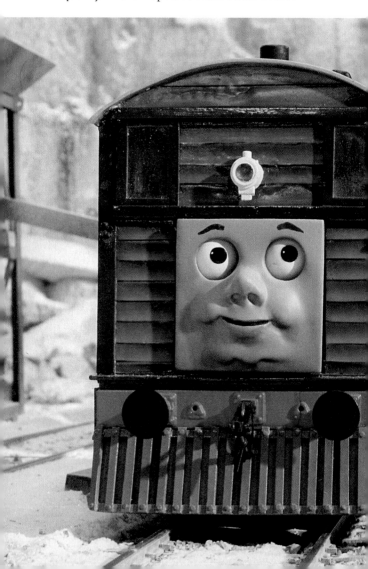

"Hmm, yes," said Toby thoughtfully.

He and his driver agreed that it would be best to help Mavis after all.

An angry farmer was telling Mavis just what she could do with her train!

"Having trouble, Mavis?" chortled Toby. "I am surprised."

"Grrr-osh!" said Mavis.

With much puffing and wheel-slip, Toby pushed Mavis and the cars back.

The hard work made his fire burn fiercely, and his fireman spread hot cinders to melt the frozen mud.

At last they were finished.

"Good-bye," called Toby. "You'll manage now, I expect."

Mavis didn't answer. She took the cars to the sheds and scuttled home to the quarry as quickly as she could.

THOMAS

EDWARD

GORDON